W9-ADL-174

02/2021

PALM BEACH COUNTY
LIBRARY SYSTEM
3650 Summit Boulevard
West Palm Beach, FL 33406-4198

Katie Woo's

❋ Neighborhood ❋

Super-Duper Librarian

by Fran Manushkin

illustrated by Laura Zarrin

PICTURE WINDOW BOOKS

a capstone imprint

Katie Woo's Neighborhood is published by
Picture Window Books, an imprint of Capstone.
1710 Roe Crest Drive
North Mankato, Minnesota 56003
www.capstonepub.com

Text © 2021 by Fran Manushkin.
Illustrations © 2021 by Capstone.

Library of Congress Cataloging-in-Publication Data
Names: Manushkin, Fran, author. | Zarrin, Laura, illustrator.
Title: Super-duper librarian / by Fran Manushkin ; illustrated by
Laura Zarrin.
Description: North Mankato, Minnesota : Picture Window Books, a
Capstone imprint, [2021] | Series: Katie Woo's neighborhood | Audience:
Ages 5–7. | Audience: Grades K–1. |
Summary: When Katie's parents take her to the library one rainy
Saturday, she finds a lot of her friends and, with the help of librarian
Miss Bliss, takes home some "super-duper" books. Includes glossary,
discussion questions, and an interview.
Identifiers: LCCN 2020025178 (print) | LCCN 2020025179 (ebook) |
ISBN 9781515882411 (library binding) | ISBN 9781515883500
(paperback) | ISBN 9781515892298 (pdf)
Subjects: CYAC: Books and reading—Fiction. | Librarians—Fiction. |
Chinese Americans—Fiction.
Classification: LCC PZ7.M3195 Mr 2021 (print) | LCC PZ7.M3195 (ebook)
| DDC [E]—dc23
LC record available at https://lccn.loc.gov/2020025178
LC ebook record available at https://lccn.loc.gov/2020025179

Designer: Bobbie Nuytten

Printed and bound in the USA. PO 3837

Table of Contents

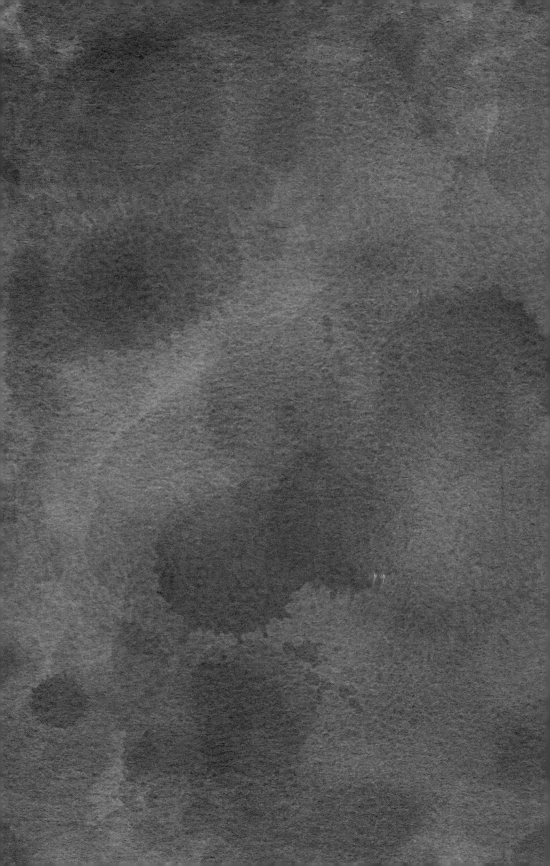

Chapter 1

A Rainy Day

It was a cold, rainy Saturday. Katie called her friends Pedro and JoJo. They weren't home.

She wondered, "What can I do today?"

"Let's go to the library,"
said Katie's dad. "I need a new
mystery."

"And I want a funny book,"
said Katie's mom.

"I'm bringing back lots of
books," said Katie. "I've read
every book in the library."

"Not yet!" Her mom smiled.
"Miss Bliss will find you more.
She's a wonderful librarian."

On the way to the library, Katie said, "I wonder where Pedro and JoJo went today. Maybe they went to the movies."

No! They were at the
library.

JoJo said, "This place is
great on a rainy day."

Pedro said, "It's great on
any day."

Chapter 2

Busy Miss Bliss

Katie saw many friends

from school. Miss Bliss was

busy checking their books

in . . .

. . . and checking books out.

Haley O'Hara and her five brothers and sisters came running in. They wanted a zillion books!

"Follow me," said Miss Bliss.

She found them books

about dragons and dinosaurs

and underwear!

Miss Bliss gave them

riddle books and pop-up

books and pigeon books.

Haley O'Hara yelled,

"Yay, Miss Bliss!"

Katie's teacher, Miss
Winkle, wanted a book
about training
her puppy.
"Have
fun!" said
Miss Bliss.

Katie told JoJo, "I want
a wonderful, fabulous,
super-duper book!"

"Me too!" said JoJo. "*Lots*
of super-duper books."

"Yikes!" Katie shouted.

"This book is about boogers!"

"Wow!" JoJo giggled.

"You can find anything in

a book!"

Roddy was a loud reader.

"SMASH! BASH! CRASH!"

His book was about racing
cars.

"Miss Bliss found this for
me," he said. "She is SO cool!"

Chapter 3
Katie's Books

Soon the library was

about to close. Katie felt sad.

"There is no super-duper

book for me."

"Wait!" said Miss Bliss.

"I've saved books for you.

I found a spooky mystery!

And here's a book in your

favorite series, Betsy-Tacy."

"SUPER-DUPER!" said Katie.

Katie added a book about

a lady explorer.

Her dad said, "You read

so many kinds of books. You

are already an explorer!"

Katie and her mom and dad hurried home.

Katie read before supper.

She read after supper.

She even took her books to bed.

When Katie fell asleep,

she had super-duper dreams.

They all had happy endings!

Glossary

explorer (ik-SPLOR-uhr)—a person who goes to an unknown place

fabulous (FAB-yuh-luhs)—very good or unusual

librarian (lye-BRER-ee-uhn)—a person who is trained in library science and helps library visitors

mystery (MISS-tur-ee)—a type of story that involves solving a crime

wonderful (WUHN-der-fuhl)—great or excellent

zillion (ZIL-yuhn)—a very large number

Katie's Questions

1. What traits make a good librarian? Would you like to be a librarian? Why or why not?

2. Imagine you are a librarian and your teacher asks for help choosing a book. What type of book would you choose for your teacher? Why?

3. A book's cover helps catch readers' attention. Draw a new cover for this book or another favorite story.

4. Write a paragraph about a librarian at your school or neighborhood library. What makes your librarian special?

5. Libraries often have special events. Imagine you were in charge of an event at the library. What is your event? Create a poster for it.

Meet the Author

Katie Interviews
a Librarian

Katie: Hi, Miss Bliss! I'm so happy I get to talk to you about being a librarian. What's your favorite thing about your job?

Miss Bliss: Well, Katie, as you might have guessed, I love helping people find books. There is nothing more fun than helping a child find the perfect book—something he or she just can't wait to get home to read.

Katie: You are really good at helping people choose books! What else do you do at work?

Miss Bliss: In addition to keeping the library organized, I order books and other reading materials for the library. I make sure we have books on a wide range of topics. In the summer, I plan a lot of special events to keep kids reading when they are out of school. We have reading contests, storytimes, and even magic and animal shows so children want to visit the library!

Katie: How did you become a librarian?

Miss Bliss: I went to college for quite a long time to become a librarian. I have my master's degree in library science. I went to college for six years in all to get that degree.

Katie: That is a lot of school. No wonder you are so smart!

Miss Bliss: I do learn a lot in this job. I'm always helping people find information and learn new things. That's bound to rub off on my brain.

Katie: Thanks again for talking to me, Miss Bliss. Now, can you help me find a book about . . . librarians?

Miss Bliss: It would be my pleasure, Katie!

About the Author

Fran Manushkin is the author of Katie Woo, the highly acclaimed fan-favorite early reader series, as well as the popular Pedro series. Her other books include *Happy in Our Skin, Baby, Come Out!* and the best-selling board books *Big Girl Panties* and *Big Boy Underpants.* There is a real Katie Woo: Fran's great-niece, who doesn't get into trouble like the Katie in the books. Fran lives in New York City, three blocks from Central Park, where she can often be found bird-watching and daydreaming. She writes at her dining room table, without the help of her two naughty cats, Chaim and Goldy.

About the Illustrator

Laura Zarrin spent her early childhood in the St. Louis, Missouri, area. There she explored creeks, woods, and attic closets, climbed trees, and dug for artifacts in the backyard, all in preparation for her future career as an archaeologist. She never became one, however, because she realized she's much happier drawing in the comfort of her own home while watching TV. When she was twelve, her family moved to the Silicon Valley in California, where she still lives with her very logical husband and teen sons, and their illogical dog, Cody.